Snowman Paul
at the Winter Olympics

Written by Yossi Lapid
Illustrated by Joanna Pasek

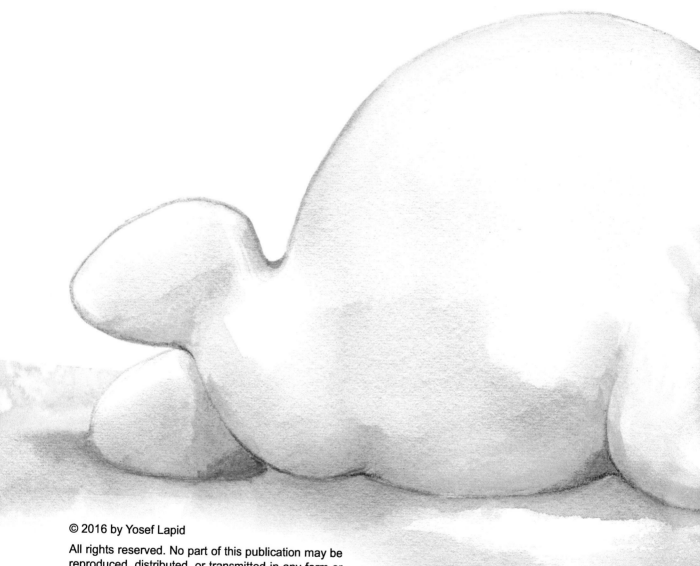

ISBN 978-0-9973899-2-0

I dedicate this book to my wonderful three children:
Ilana, Lior and Talia. You are the true inspiration for
Snowman Paul and this book series.

I knew my Paul was very clever,
Perhaps the smartest snowman ever.

So I was shocked when I was told
He planned to win Olympic gold.

"Paul," I said, "you're much too old
To win a silver or a gold.
Besides, it's risky, you might fall.
So let's forget about it, Paul!"

"Me fall?" laughed Paul. "Now that's bizarre.
How silly you poor humans are!
How can a snowman trip on snow?
Well, are you coming?

Time to go!"

What could I do? I had to go
With my swell-headed-pile-of-snow,

But I was sure that very soon
He'd fizzle like a popped balloon.

But, as it happened, I was wrong;
Paul's scores were extremely strong.

In ski-jumping he jumped so far
They had to fetch him with a car!

In speed-skating, he raced so fast
You'd think he rode an Arctic blast!

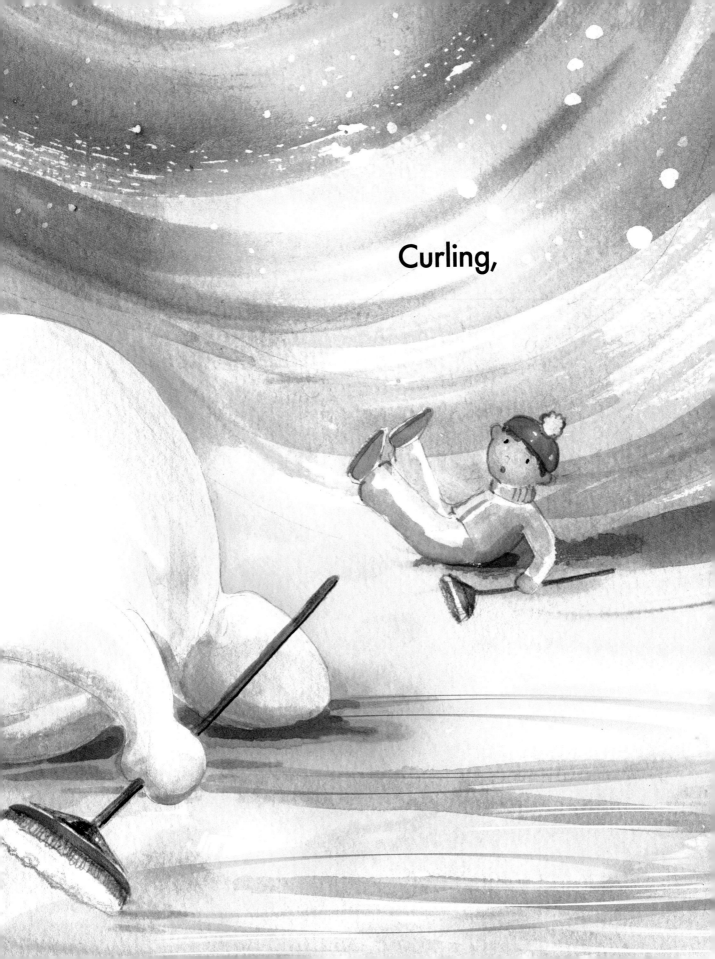

Curling,

Snowboard,

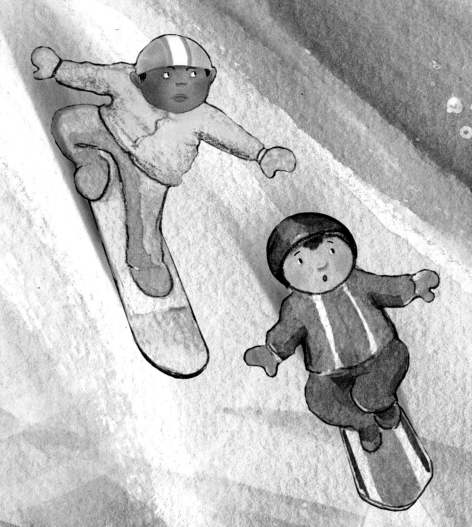

The luge-run,
Guess who, each time, was

Number One?

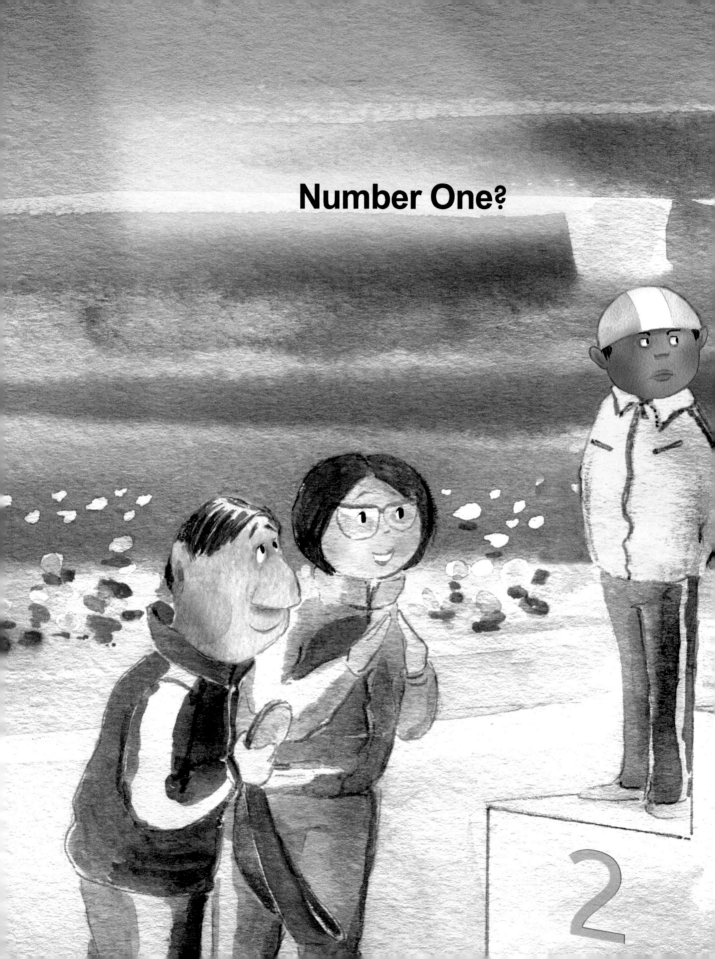

Paul was as proud as one could be,
But something looked fishy to me...

His friends — the wind, the ice, the snow —
Kept helping my Paul steal the show!

"Paul," I yelled, "why did you cheat —
I saw you clearly from my seat..."

"No way," snapped Paul. "That isn't true!"

"I'd tell the truth if I were you!"

So, we went home and drank hot fudge...

But Paul still keeps a little grudge,
For now, he solemnly proclaims,
"Just wait until those Summer Games..."

69178867R00027